BEFORE YOU CAME

By Patricia MacLachlan & Emily MacLachlan Charest

Illustrated by David Diaz

KATHERINE TEGEN BOOKS
An Imprint of HarperCollins Publishers

Katherine Tegen Books is an imprint of HarperCollins Publishers.

Before You Came

Library of Congress Cataloging-in-Publication Data

MacLachlan, Patricia.

Before you came / by Patricia MacLachlan and Emily MacLachlan Charest ; illustrated by David Diaz. —— 1st ed.

p.   cm.

Summary: A mother relates how she spent time before her child arrived, then passes on a gift of days paddling a red canoe, reading in a pillow-filled

hammock until dark, and watching the moon rise at night.

ISBN 978-0-06-051234-7 (trade bdg.) —— ISBN 978-0-06-051235-4 (lib. bdg.)

[1. Amusements——Fiction.   2. Mother and child——Fiction.]   I. Charest, Emily MacLachlan.   II. Diaz, David, ill.   III. Title.

PZ7.M2225Bef   2011   2009024459

[E]——dc22   CIP

                                                                                                                                                                                                  AC

Typography by Martha Rago

11 12 13 14 15 SCP 10 9 8 7 6 5 4 3 2 1

❖

First Edition

Before you came, I had a house by the river with a porch wrapped around.

I had a red canoe. When I paddled downriver, swallows dipped and swooped, catching bugs just above the water.

Before you came, I had a
garden of blue morning glories,
red zinnias, and Russian sage
against a gray wall.

At night my moonflower bloomed for just one night, unfolding like butterfly wings.

Before you came, I had a cat named Sofia. She was nice some of the time.

One day she brought me three kittens, one
by one by one, gray and black and orange.

I had a dog named Rudy. He chased squirrels and came back so I could tell him he was the nicest dog in the world. Which he was.

Before you came, I had birds at my feeders—
cardinals and finches and nuthatches.

Blue jays and doves.

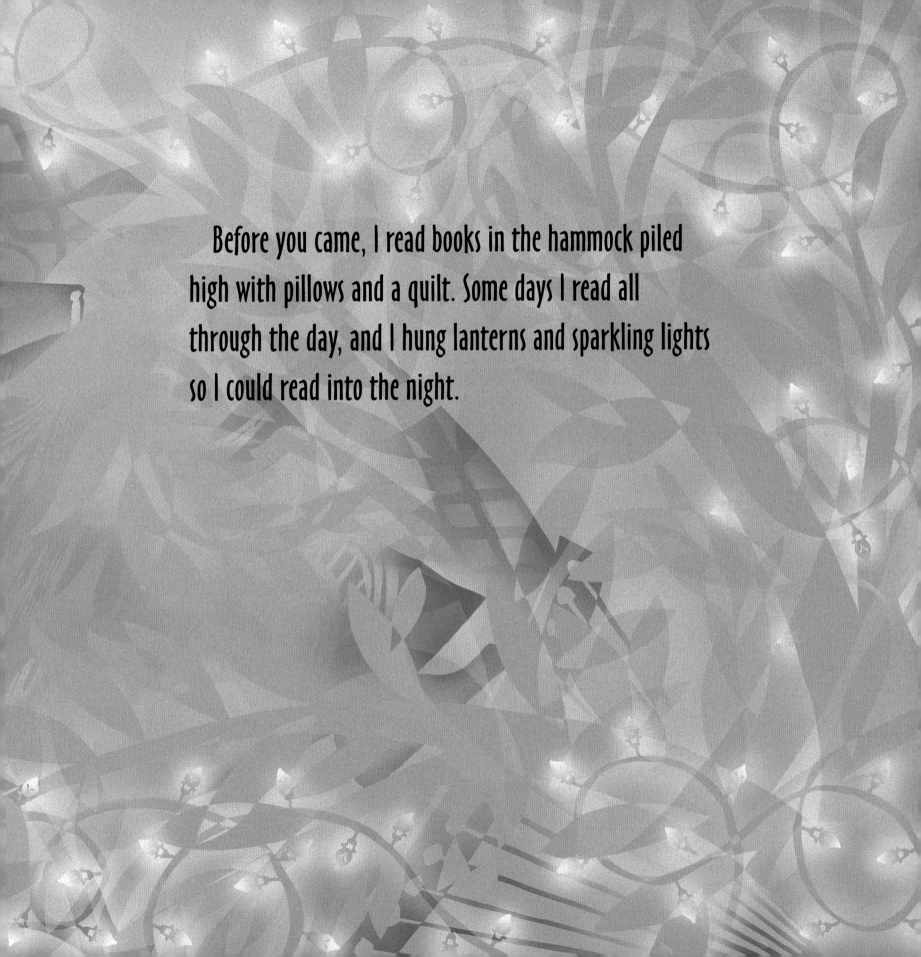

Before you came, I read books in the hammock piled high with pillows and a quilt. Some days I read all through the day, and I hung lanterns and sparkling lights so I could read into the night.

Before you came, I had music. Your father played the guitar for me. He wrote songs that made me laugh.

Some nights the moon came up
orange,
then yellow,
then white.

Then you were born.

And now all the things I had before you came
are for you.

You can watch the river pass by.
You can ride in the red canoe.
You can watch the moonflower bloom.
The cat will make you smile.
The dog will keep you safe.

You can read books. All day long.
All night long if you want.

Your father will sing you to sleep.
And you can watch the moon come up
orange,
then yellow,
then white.

I used to think I
had everything.
And now I do.
I have you.